O9-AIF-145

Goodnight, My Angel

A LULLABYE

BILLY JOEL

ILLUSTRATED BY YVONNE GILBERT

SCHOLASTIC PRESS · NEW YORK

A Byron Preiss Book

Library of Congress Cataloging-in-Publication Data available

ISBN 0-439-55376-8

10 9 8 7 6 5 4 3 2 1   04 05 06 07 08

Printed in Singapore 46
First edition, October 2004

The text and display type was set in Mrs. Eaves
The illustrations were done in colored pencil on paper
Book design by Elizabeth B. Parisi and 27.12 Design Ltd., NYC

To My Darling Daughter, Alexa

— B.J.

This one's for Danny

— Y.G.

Goodnight, my angel,
time to close your eyes and
save these questions for another day.

*I think I know
what you've
been asking me.*

I think you know
what I've been
trying to say.

I promised I would
never leave you.

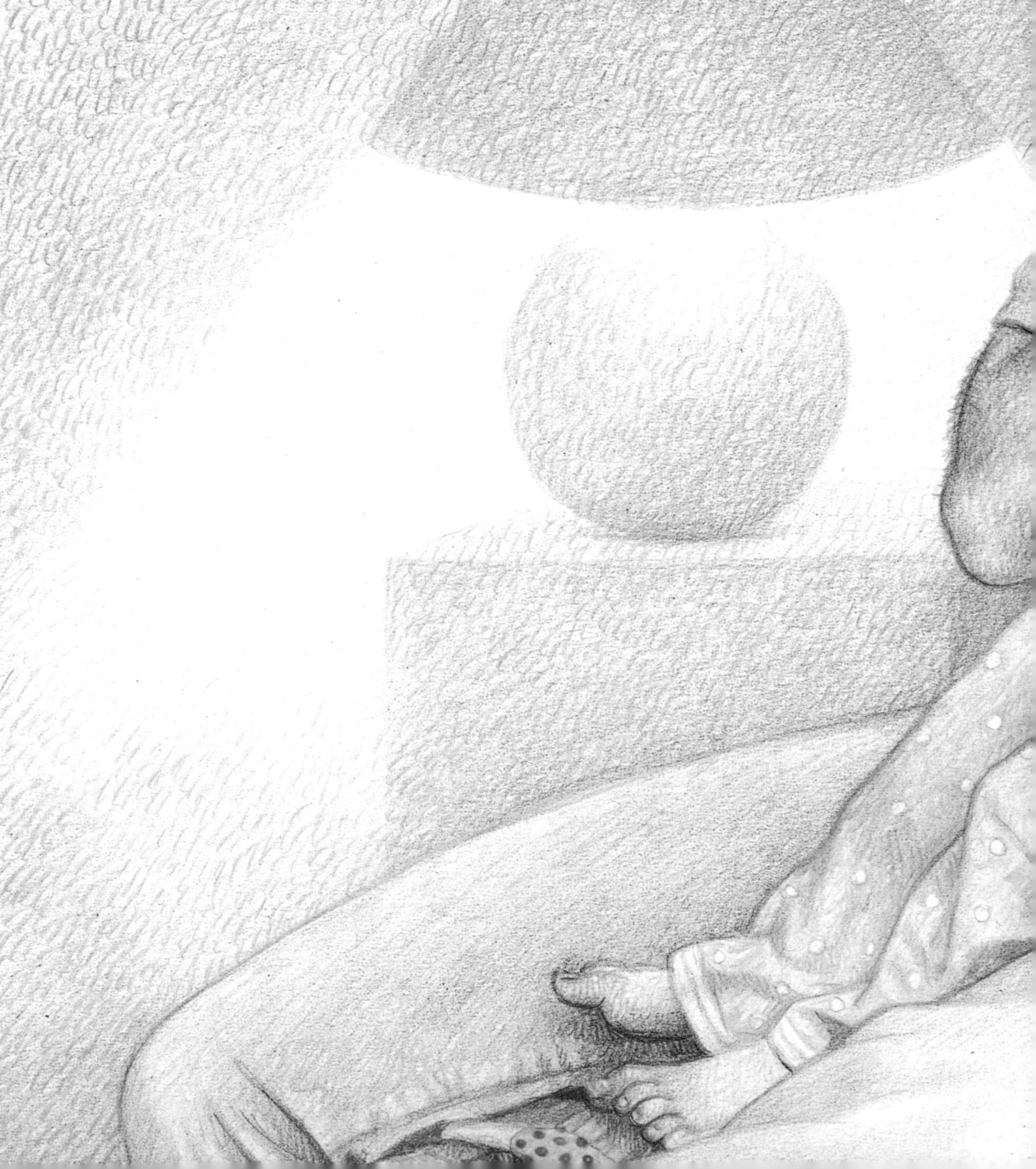

And you should always know
wherever you may go,

no matter

where you are,

I never will be

far away.

Goodnight, my angel,
now it's time to sleep.
And still so many things
I want to say.

Remember
all the songs
you sang for me
when we went
sailing on
an emerald bay.

And like a boat
out on the ocean,
I'm rocking you
to sleep.

The water's dark,

and deep inside

this ancient heart

you'll always be

a part of me.

Goodnight, my angel,

now it's time to dream.

And dream how wonderful

your life will be.

Someday your child

may cry,

and if you sing

this lullabye,

then in your heart

there will always be a part of me.

Someday we'll all be gone.

But lullabies go on and on....

They never die.

That's how

you and I will be.

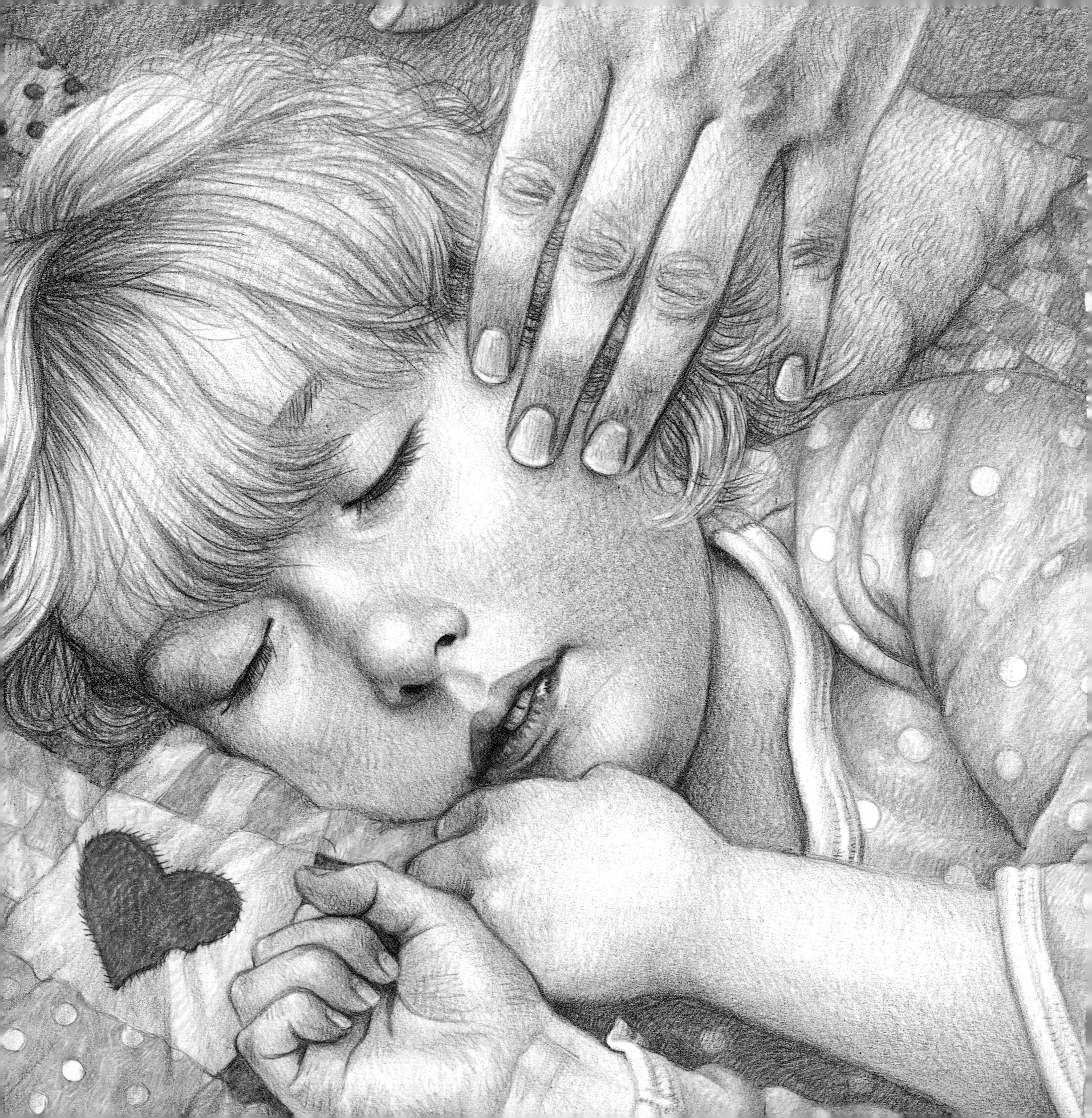